Dead
Trouble
Keith Gray

illustrated by
CLIVE SCRUTON

mammoth

First published in Great Britain in 1997 by Mammoth
an imprint of Reed International Books Limited
Michelin House, 81 Fulham Road, London SW3 6RB
and Auckland and Melbourne

Text copyright © 1997 Keith Gray
Illustrations copyright © 1997 Clive Scruton

The rights of Keith Gray and Clive Scruton to be
identified as the author and illustrator of this work have
been asserted by them in accordance with the
Copyright, Designs and Patents Act 1988

ISBN 0 7497 2888 4

10 9 8 7 6 5 4 3 2 1

A CIP catalogue record for this book is
available from the British Library

Printed in Great Britain by Cox & Wyman Ltd,
Reading, Berkshire

One

SEAN SAW IT first. He almost stepped on it, but flinched his foot away quicker than if it had been dog-muck.

'Jaz!' he shouted. 'Jaz, look at this.'

Jarrod was ahead of him, walking away up the street.

Sean's small, ginger head bobbed enthusiastically. 'Hey, Jaz,' he called again. 'Come and look at this. Quick!'

Jarrod half turned but carried on walking. His mother was going to kill him, though he reckoned it was all her fault anyway. Jarrod didn't have many friends, you see, and it was all because his mother was a head teacher. How many kids wanted to play with the head teacher's son? How many kids wanted to tell the head teacher's son their secrets, or let him into their gang? Jarrod only knew one, and that was Sean. All the other kids picked on him and called him 'Brains' or 'Prof' because of his glasses. Sean had lots of friends at school, he was always playing football with them, and sometimes Jarrod just wished he could be a bit more like him. Unfortunately, being like Sean could often lead to trouble, and Jarrod's mother was not going to like the idea of his second set of lines this week: *I must not talk or play the fool during lessons, but must leave my antics until break-time.*

'It's a gun, Jaz!'

This time Jarrod listened. He spun round and raced to the spot where Sean was pointing. His schoolbag lay discarded and for-  gotten on the pavement. 'It's a gun,' he said. He sounded as if he didn't believe his own words.

'I told you.'

It was a revolver, a six shooter, dull grey with a round barrel bit in the middle where the bullets went. Just like the one cowboys used, except it had a shorter muzzle.

Jarrod snatched it up quickly and stuffed it away inside his coat.

'Hey!' Sean was deeply offended. 'It's mine. I saw it first.' He rose to his full height of a couple of centimetres taller than Jarrod and grabbed his friend's arm.

Jarrod tried to push him away. 'Do you want everyone to know?' he hissed. 'Half the street would be here in a minute if they saw us.'

Sean backed down quickly. Why hadn't he thought of that? He glanced at all the net-curtained windows. He hated making a fool of himself in front of Jarrod. Tallow was only a small village. In a place like this it was your right to know everyone's business.

'What d'you think we should do with it?' he said.

'Let's take it to the den.'

The den lay at the back of the allot-

ments, right at the edge of the fields. The shed was battered and rotting, and the door had to be physically lifted into its hole because of a broken top hinge, but the two friends never noticed that sort of thing. Inside, the shelves were littered with bags of fertiliser, packets of seeds and broken plant pots. Only one shelf had been cleared and on this sat two torches,

The Big Book of Spies by Giles Brandreth, and an old lacquered music box, which was used for hiding anything secret. Since 5 November it had remained empty, but right now it seemed the perfect place for their latest find.

The allotments were virtually empty as the two boys skittered down the path in between Mr Rider's carrots and Old Man

Cooney's potatoes. Jarrod unhooked the rusty padlock that never quite closed and they darted inside, struggling as always to shut the door behind them.

Jarrod took his hand out from underneath his coat and knelt down, placing the gun on one of the stained, grey carpet tiles. He was glad to let go of it.

Sean's fingers hovered about it excitedly, but he still didn't touch it.

'It is real, isn't it?'

'Yeah.'

Sean grinned. 'I knew it was.'

'I wonder if it's the farmer's?' Jarrod said. 'He uses guns all the time to shoot rabbits.'

Sean was quiet. He shrugged. 'I reckon

it's a cowboy's gun,' he said.

Jarrod nodded.

'I can't wait to tell everyone at school.'

'You can't!' Jarrod almost shouted.

'But . . .'

'They'll tell my mum, and she'll take it off us. No one else is allowed to know. We've got to keep it secret.'

They both looked at the music box.

They both looked at the gun.

'I wonder if it's loaded?' Jarrod said.

'Of course it's loaded. All guns are loaded.'

'Not always.'

'This one is. I bet you.'

Jarrod pushed his glasses up his nose. He looked at his friend nervously. 'There's only one way to find out.'

Sean looked up suddenly. His face broke into a huge grin.

They checked the allotments quickly, peeping around to make sure no one was there, then darted outside. They pushed through the bushes behind the den and raced down into the ditch-like banks of the stream that separated the allotments from the fields. Jarrod carried the gun inside the box. They vaulted the stream and climbed the embankment on the

other side, then sprinted across the open field. The springtime youthfulness of the crop did nothing to hide them, so speed was essential. The copse of trees was at least two hundred metres away, but they had made this run loads of times before.

'Are you sure . . . this'll be all right?' Sean panted.

'Yeah . . . Everyone will just think . . . it's the farmer shooting rabbits.'

'What if we're seen?'

'No one will see us if we're quick.'

The revolver thunked and clunked in its box.

The copse itself was fairly dense and it took all their strength to fight their way through the branches and bracken at ground level. Jarrod suddenly remembered that he was supposed to be home on time. He knew there'd be big trouble when he faced his mother, but he pushed the thought to the back of his mind. At the moment all he could think about was the gun.

The two boys scrapped and scrabbled with the branches. They ducked in between the trees, dodging their overhanging limbs, and waded through the foliage towards the tiny clearing at the centre of the copse.

Jarrod unzipped his coat, then gently took out the wooden box and placed it on the ground. Carefully, he opened the lid and very slowly lifted out the gun. He held it out towards Sean, who shuffled quickly to his left to avoid the barrel.

'Do you want to fire it?' Jarrod asked.

Sean watched the gun. Oh boy, did he want to shoot it! He would give anything to pull the trigger, but he was frightened he'd do it wrong, he'd make a fool of himself. So he'd let his friend shoot it first. Jaz would know how to do it properly, and then Sean would copy what he did.

'Nah, I'm not bothered,' he lied. 'I'll let you shoot it first.'

'OK, then.'

Jarrod got to his feet and pushed his finger through the trigger guard, settling the handle against his palm. It felt clumsy. He wished Sean would fire it first, but he didn't want Sean to think he was chicken.

He pointed the gun at a tree with ivy twisting round its trunk. He pushed his glasses slowly up his nose. He held his arm outstretched, his body turned at a right angle, leaning away from the gun, and squeezed the trigger back. His finger began to ache as the hammer pulled itself slowly back.

The hammer clicked down, a split second of the purest silence . . .

And the world exploded. A burst of

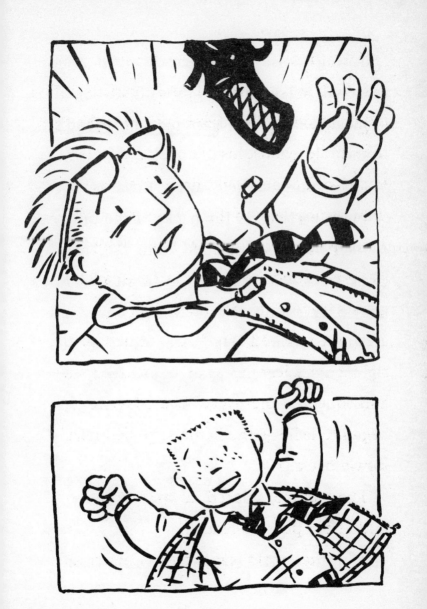

flashing noise and Jarrod's arm was thrown back at his shoulder. Sean squealed as the gun leapt from his friend's hand.

The noise rolled away towards the clouds, carried on the backs of the birds, which had been startled from the trees. The boys were almost too frightened to move. A strange sickly feeling coiled in Jarrod's stomach. He looked down at the

gun lying in the grass and listened to the birds circling in the sky.

Sean was jumping up and down with excitement. 'I told you it had bullets,' he was saying. 'I told you so. That was ace.'

'Yeah,' Jarrod said.

'Quick. Let's have a go.'

Jarrod kept his voice low, everything around him seemed to be watching, listening. 'Come on, we'd better get going.

Someone might come.'

'But I haven't had my turn yet.'

'The farmer might catch us.'

'You said he wouldn't see us.'

'That was before we made all that noise.'

Jarrod knelt down and picked up the revolver. He played his fingers along the warm barrel.

'You missed the tree, Jaz,' Sean called. 'I bet I could hit a tree. Can I shoot it tonight?'

'OK,' Jarrod said, and he put the gun back into the box and closed the lid.

Two

SEAN RAN ACROSS the road and headed through the tall, wrought-iron gates into the allotments. He sprinted down the path towards the shed, nearly knocking Old Man Cooney right off his bike.

'Whoa there, lad,' the old man cried as he braked sharply, planting his boots firmly on the path. 'What's your hurry?'

'Sorry, Mr Cooney,' Sean puffed. 'I'm meeting Jaz in the den.'

'Aye.' Mr Cooney nodded, hawked and

spat on to the mud, all in one practised motion. 'I saw your friend come. He's a quiet one, isn't he?'

Sean shrugged. His feet itched to be moving again.

'I hope you're looking after your grandfather's shed,' Mr Cooney said.

'Oh yeah,' Sean replied. 'We keep it just how he used to have it.'

'I'm glad to hear it. He looked after his plot well, did your grandad.' He rocked the rusty pedal of his bike back up into its pinnacle position under his left boot. 'And how's your mother these days?'

'OK.' Sean held his face down.

'Still havin' trouble with that foreign bloke of hers, is she?'

'My dad's American.' Sean couldn't look the old man in the eyes.

'Aye, your grandad said she'd have trouble with that one.' He wagged an old cracked finger at the boy. 'Just you mind that mother of yours. She's a good woman, she is.'

'And my father's a good man,' Sean hissed under his breath, but Mr Cooney was already pushing his bicycle away through the gates.

Sean clenched his hands in anger as the old man rode away unsteadily. He hated the nosey old man.

Jarrod was sitting on the floor of the den when Sean burst through the door.

Jarrod was the first to speak. 'I just realised something at tea that we never thought of.'

'What's that?'

Jarrod took the revolver out from the music box and Sean noticed that it had been opened somehow. The fat round bit in the middle that held the bullets (he didn't know what its proper name was) had been popped out and Jarrod showed him that all the spaces were filled with a bullet, apart from one.

'How did you open it?' Sean asked.

'I just pulled this and it clicked out.' Jarrod showed him. 'This came out too.' Jarrod showed him the empty cartridge.

'Cool. Let's see it.'

But Jarrod ignored him. He placed the cartridge back in the music box. 'See what I mean?' he continued. He pointed at the bullets. 'We've only got five left now. It's a six shooter and we've already used one. We've got to save the rest for really special occasions.'

'But I haven't had a go yet.'

'Yeah, I know. But we can't waste them.'

'Can't I even have my turn? You said I could shoot it tonight. You shot it, so why can't I?'

'I didn't say that you couldn't.' Jarrod tried to placate his friend. 'I just think that we should save the bullets.'

'I don't think it's fair.'

Jarrod shrugged, putting the gun back in the box. 'So what did Cooney want?' he asked, changing the subject.

'He was calling my dad a foreigner and

saying that he was no good for my mum.'

'Are your mum and dad still arguing a lot?'

'Loads. My dad wants to go back to America, but my mum wants to stay here.'

'Would you go?'

Sean shrugged. He didn't want to talk about it. There was a brief but uncomfortable silence between the boys.

'I've got to go home,' Jarrod said. 'My mum's going mad because of my lines.' He'd been staring at the gun, but now he covered it with the lid and stood up. He placed the box on the shelf behind some dead plants in tatty plastic pots.

They walked home along the side of the stream. It led all the way to the back of

Jarrod's house. Jarrod climbed the fence to drop over into his back garden.

'Wild West,' Sean shouted.

'What do you mean?' Jarrod sat astride the top of the fence.

'That's our secret password,' Sean said. 'For our cowboy gang.'

'Yeah, OK,' Jarrod grinned. 'Wild West.' Then he jumped into the garden.

Sean didn't want to return home straight away. His parents would probably be shouting at each other anyway. He'd just be in the way, getting on their nerves.

He sat himself down on the lip of the stream and dangled the toe of his trainer in the water, causing a little break in its flow. They'd definitely be arguing. He knew that for sure. Or his dad would be sulking. It was better when his dad sulked, because then at least there was no shouting. He hated it when they shouted at him. They shouted at him for the tiniest of reasons nowadays. Like leaving his bike out in the rain, or not hanging his clothes up properly.

The breeze was starting to nip, so he pulled his coat tighter around himself and zipped up the front. His parents never did anything together any more. If Dad put a video on, Mum would watch the telly in another room. If Mum went out into the garden, Dad came indoors or went into the shed. It hadn't always been like that. Sean remembered long days out in the car, like the time they'd gone to see Bamford Castle. Sean had told his dad all about Robin Hood because they'd been reading about him at school. Dad had told Sean all about Butch Cassidy and the Sundance Kid. Sean liked Dad's stories about America. His favourite was the one about Billy the Kid robbing the stage coach in Dodge City. But his dad never told him stories any more.

Sean kicked savagely at the water, splashing cold droplets into the toes of his trainers. How could he choose? He loved Mum just as much as he loved Dad. He kicked again, the icy water spraying his exposed socks. Why should he choose? No one could make him. His trousers were now wet and his legs began to feel cold. Why couldn't his mum and dad stay together?

Life wasn't fair.

And why wouldn't Jaz let him shoot the gun? It was his turn.

Well, stuff Jaz. And stuff them all. Everyone. He'd shoot the gun if he wanted to. After all, he'd found it.

It was dark by the time he reached the allotments. Once inside the den he illuminated the place with the two torches, laying them on separate shelves on either side of the shed to push their light into the centre. He liked the way the shadows looked; like a film effect, how shadows should really look.

He only realised he was shaking slightly when he reached across to take the music box down from its perch. He fumbled to undo the catch. His heart thumped as he pushed the lid back to reveal the gun. He felt guilty. He knew Jaz had told him not to fire it. But it was his turn. Jaz shouldn't have been allowed to back out of his

promise. And, anyway, Sean knew how to
fire a gun better than Jaz. Jaz had just
pulled the trigger. Sean knew you had to
click the hammer bit back first. You had to
pull it back into its cocked position before
you pulled the trigger. No wonder Jaz had
missed the tree.

The gun was heavier than he'd

expected. And colder. The metal of the barrel was really cold to touch. But it felt good. Hard. Solid. It was a little large for his hand, but he could hold it well enough. Cocking the hammer was awkward, it was really stiff. He struggled to manage it, but once it was done he was ready.

He looked around the den for something to shoot at. His eyes fell on the Giles Brandreth book. The pointy hat made the spy on the cover look a bit like a cowboy. He propped the book up against one of the bags of peat and positioned a torch on a shelf opposite so that the target was spotlit. He positioned himself so that he didn't block the torch's beam, so that it shone from over his left shoulder. Slowly, he raised the gun in both hands, aiming it exactly at the body of the spy.

He was still shaking. The gun's sight jigged around the book's cover. He gripped the cold metal tighter, squinting one eye shut. He was determined to get his aim perfect.

He took a deep breath. He was Billy the Kid.

There was a sudden thumping on the shed door.

'Hey? Who's in there?'

Sean almost dropped the gun in surprise. Then he tripped over his own feet as he hurried to grab the music box, switch off the torches and hide the gun all at the same time.

There was another thump on the door, another shout, and then Old Man Cooney waded into the dim interior of the den. His face looked redder than ever. He glanced about quickly, his eyes darting around the shelves and walls. He finally looked at Sean nervously getting to his knees and then his feet.

'I wondered who was in here at this time,' the old man said. 'I thought it might be some vandals pinching your grandad's stuff and writing filth on the walls.' He stepped further aside, watching the young boy. 'They've done it before, to Tom Colly, you know. I nearly got the little so and so's that time, but . . .' He paused. His baggy eyes narrowed. 'Now what's that you've got there, son?'

Sean didn't answer. He took a tentative step backwards. His heart was still hammering in his chest, and now it was about to start thundering in fear of being caught with the gun.

'That had better not be one of them big marker pens, laddy, or you're for the high jump.' He took a step closer to the boy, who backed away. 'C'mon. Behind your back. I know you've got something there.'

Sean was trapped. He couldn't go any-
where. He was quite literally backed into a
corner. He frantically tried shoving the

gun down the back of his trousers.

'I'm talking to you, boy.' He took hold of Sean's arm. 'If you've been the one writing filth around here then I'll . . .' The old man yanked on Sean's arm just as the boy had pushed the muzzle into the top of his belt, but he lost his grip on it.

The gun clunked to the floor.

They both looked at it.

The old man bent over, squinting in the grubby light to see what it was. 'That's no marker pen.' He sounded disappointed, then suddenly caught his breath as he realised what it really was.

Sean was quick to snatch the gun back. He wanted to edge his way round the old man and run out of the door to freedom, but his broad figure completely blocked the way.

'Let me see that again. You just show that to me right now, laddy.'

Sean shook his head. 'No.'

'Boys've no business with things like that.'

Sean was desperate. If he gave up the gun, not only would he get himself into a whole heap of trouble, but he'd never be able to shoot it either. And he really wanted to shoot it. He looked over Old Man Cooney's shoulder, at the shed door hanging open off its broken hinge.

The old man reached for him.

Clutching the gun to his chest, Sean put his head down and barged past, banging the shelf, knocking a flowerpot and *The Big Book of Spies* to the floor as he ran.

Three

JARROD WAS READING in his bedroom. He'd just reached a really excit-
ing point in the book when he heard a
sharp tapping on his window. He dropped
the book immediately. It could only be
one person: Sean.

He pulled open the curtain to see his
friend clutching the drainpipe. He looked
frantic.

'Open the window,' Sean mouthed, still
tapping. 'Open the window,' and Jarrod
was quick to undo the catch. 'We've got to

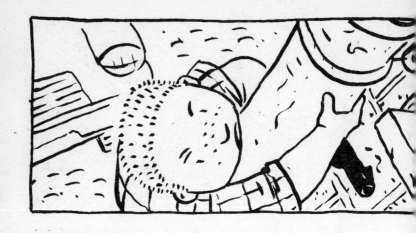

go,' Sean said. 'Quick. Come on. We've got to get out of here.'

'What's wrong? What's happened?'

Sean didn't answer, he was already climbing back down.

'What's going on, Sean?' he asked nervously.

'Old Man Cooney,' he called up quietly. 'He saw me.' He waved the gun, which he'd had stuffed down the front of his

trousers. 'He's seen the gun. We've got to get going or they'll take it off us.'

Jarrod still didn't move.

The two boys looked at each other. Jarrod, leaning out of his bedroom window; Sean, clutching the drainpipe. They were both silent.

Sean shrugged, then lowered himself quickly to the ground. He glanced around the dark garden, checking over both

shoulders, then stuffed the pistol down
the front of his trousers. He looked back
up at his friend.

'Come on, Jaz.'

'I can't, Sean.'

'Listen,' Sean said, checking over his
shoulder again. 'If we stay, we get into
trouble, right? Big trouble. 'Cos Old Man

Cooney's seen the gun. But if we run away, then we can think about what to do.'

Jarrod nodded. It seemed to make sense in the heat of the moment. He knew that everybody would want to take the gun away from them, and he desperately didn't want that. The gun was the first special thing that had ever happened to him. But he couldn't run away, could he? When he was little he had dreamt of running away and finding a mother who wasn't a head teacher, one who had a massive family with loads of brothers and sisters for him to play with. But it had only ever been a daydream.

Sean was getting more and more edgy. 'Come on then. D'you want to get caught or what? I'll go without you.' He hopped from one foot to the other in a little nervous jig.

'I mean it,' Sean said. 'I'll go without you. I really will.'

'I can't.'

And when Jarrod didn't move Sean shouted, 'Get lost then. Stuff you. Great friend you are.'

Sean took a running jump at the high fence to get over it as quickly as possible. Jarrod watched him go, knowing he'd let his best friend down. But he was still too scared to follow him. Suddenly he hated himself. He'd lost the gun and his friend. He'd probably never see either of them again.

He ran over to his wardrobe, grabbed his coat . . . but couldn't muster up enough courage to put it on. He caught sight of his reflection in the mirror on his wardrobe door. 'Wimp,' he hissed, and sneered at himself angrily.

'JAZ! JAZ!'

Jarrod literally dived across his bed to the window. Sean was back in the garden, looking more panicky than ever.

'I've just seen Old Man Cooney,' he shouted up. 'He's coming to your house. My dad's there too.'

'Where are they? Where did you see them?' Jarrod was panicking now.

'Coming up the road. I've just seen them.'

This time Jarrod didn't hesitate. He was quick climbing out of the window, but even quicker following Sean over the

fence at the bottom of the garden and into
the darkness of the fields beyond.

Four

THE BRITTLE CHUNKS of earth crunched and crushed underneath their shoes as they ran. Jarrod followed Sean. Sean followed his feet. The bright full moon lit their way across the fields.

All Sean could think about was running away. It was best to run away. At least that's what he'd decided. He reckoned that if he ran away he wouldn't get into trouble. If he ran away he'd be able to keep the gun, and he'd be able to shoot it. There was no way he was going to let Old

Man Cooney or anyone else get their hands on it. It was his. And Jarrod's.

The field rose and fell like the camber of a massive road. It was separated from the next by a ditch and a hedge. The ditch was easy enough to jump but the sharp tangled hedge pulled at their clothes and scratched their hands as they clambered through. The next field was full of sheep, all huddled together, sleeping. The boys woke them up as they ran by, startled

bleats making them jump as the massed wool trundled noisily away on dozens of legs.

Jarrod was excited, but frightened too. This was it. He was actually running away. How many times had he imagined doing this in the past? And now he really, truly was doing it. But, unlike Sean, he had no misconceptions about it getting them out of trouble. He knew that by running away the pair of them were actually landing

themselves even deeper in trouble. And that was why he didn't stop to think about it. That was why he kept on running.

Through another hedge and across another ditch, the next field rose up into a hill. Sean and Jarrod panted their way to the top, to a lone tree with bare, twisted

branches. Here they allowed themselves to
rest a while. They turned around to look
back at the lights of the village a kilometre
or so away.

'I wonder what Cooney's told my mum
and dad,' Jarrod said. 'I bet it's all lies. I
bet he's made it sound really bad.'

Sean didn't answer. He just stared at the lights.

'They'll be looking for us by now,' Jarrod said.

Sean nodded. 'Yeah, but they're not gonna find us. Not where we're going.'

'Where are we going?' Jarrod asked.

Sean spun around quickly on his heels, turning his back on the glow from the village. He squinted his eyes as he scanned the moonlit fields beyond. 'What about them woods over there?' He pointed out the dark outline of the trees three or four fields away. 'They'd be dead cool. We could build a fire and make a den in the trees.'

Jarrod wasn't so sure, but he was tired

so he agreed anyway.

'We'd be just like cowboys,' Sean said.

'Cowboys don't live in the woods.'

'How do you know?'

'I've never seen one film where cowboys have lived in a wood.'

'Yeah, but that's in films. What about real life? And anyway,' Sean took out the gun from its snug place tucked down the front of his trousers, 'we've got a real cowboy gun, so now we're cowboys too.'

Jarrod nodded and giggled. He held out his hand. 'Here, let me carry it.'

Sean shook his head. 'You always carry it. It's my turn now.' Ignoring Jarrod's grumbling complaints, he held it high above his head and ran down the hill towards the wood. But once he'd started running, he couldn't stop. He ran faster and faster. He ran so fast his legs couldn't keep up with the rest of his body. As he hurtled down the hill they buckled underneath him and he sprawled face first on to the ground, flinging his arms in front of himself, letting go of the gun.

'Idiot,' Jarrod hissed at Sean, making his way carefully down to where his friend had fallen. 'Now look what you've done.' He dropped to his knees and started searching for the pistol, running his hands over the uneven ground and tossing any large chunks of earth aside. 'No wonder I didn't want you to have it. First you let Old Man Cooney see it, and now you've lost it.'

'Wasn't my fault,' Sean mumbled.

It took them at least quarter of an hour to find the gun, and then Jarrod kept hold of it. They were both angry with each other. Neither of them spoke as they started walking again. It was turning chilly, the wind was picking up, and they

were both tired. The furrows made walking awkward and clumsy.

'I'm tired.'

'I'm cold.'

'Me too.'

Before they reached the wood they joined up with a small dirt track that ran along the side of a narrow hushed stream. Jarrod wondered if it was the same one that ran through the village. The track

turned and crossed the stream and the two boys followed it all the way up to the dark edge of the wood where the trees were dense and the spaces between very black.

The earlier argument was forgotten as they carefully moved from the open field into the crowded wood. They stayed close together, almost creeping along. The branches made a tight, net-like cover above their heads. Only tiny glimpses of light filtered through.

'How far in should we go?' Jarrod asked.

'Not far,' Sean said. 'We just need to find a place big enough to build a fire.'

Jarrod nodded.

They found a grassy patch and quickly gathered twigs and broken branches for a fire, but without any matches neither of them knew how to get one going. They'd both heard stories about boy scouts rubbing sticks together, but when it came to putting this into practice they found it completely impossible.

'That's not the way to do it.'

'You try it, if you're so clever.'

'Give me the sticks then.'

'Get your own sticks.'

The adventure soon began to lose its glamour, its magic. The cold was eager to snatch it away, whilst the dark was content to let it seep slowly out of them and into its shadows. And that's always the dangerous part, because you never can trust a shadow once it's mixed with a bit of magic.

They sat together, shivering, tired, watching the shadows of the trees lurch and creep in the breeze.

'It'll be better in the morning,' Sean said.

Jarrod didn't reply. He clutched the gun tightly as he hugged his knees to his chest, but he was no warmer than the ground he was sitting on. He wished he knew what Old Man Cooney had told his parents. He could just imagine the look on his mother's face when she realised he'd run away.

'It'll be dawn soon. We'll be able to see

properly then. We'll be able to find proper
sticks for a fire.'

Jarrod slowly nodded his head.

Suddenly, Sean jumped to his feet. 'We
still ought to celebrate,' he said. He
grinned hugely at Jarrod, hoping his

friend could see it in the dark. 'You know, our first day of freedom and everything.'

Jarrod was quiet. He was drained of energy. He just couldn't stop thinking about his parents. They'd probably check the den first. He wondered if he'd made his mum cry.

'Come on,' Sean said. 'We ought to fire the gun. As a celebration.' He mimed holding and firing the gun. 'Wild West!' he

shouted and made a gunshot noise with his mouth.

'No.' Jarrod shook his head. 'We can't waste the bullets.'

'Come on. Don't be boring.'

'No.'

'It's my gun as well. I found it.' He stood glaring at Jarrod, who simply remained quiet. 'It's not just your gun. You don't own it.' Jarrod didn't answer. 'Give

me it,' Sean told him.

Jarrod bunched himself up even tighter. 'I'm going home tomorrow, Sean. In the morning.'

'You can't!'

'I have to.'

'But I thought we were going to be cow-boys.'

'We can't stay here for ever. You must come home too.'

'Get lost. No way. We'll get into trouble.' Sean started pacing the clearing. 'And they'll take the gun off us. Don't you want the gun any more?'

Jarrod shrugged. 'My mum and dad will be looking for me,' he said. 'Yours will too.'

'Tough. Let them. They don't care about me anyway.'

'They'll send the police and everything after us. The longer we wait, the more trouble we'll be in.'

'Some friend you are!' Sean shouted. He slumped himself down into a heap with his back to Jarrod. He was shivering.

Jarrod watched his friend's back shuddering. He couldn't tell if Sean was crying or not, but he was too exhausted to argue any more.

Sean *was* crying, but there was no way he was going to admit it to Jarrod. He didn't even really know why he was crying. He felt like a complete wimp. He rocked himself slightly, his whole body tense, ready, waiting to explode. He wanted to scream. At Jarrod. At Old Man Cooney. At his mum and dad.

After a while the tears subsided. He was silent, rocking and brooding, thinking. Could he run away on his own? Why not? At least then there'd be *no one* to tell him what to do. All he'd wanted was to shoot the gun. It wasn't fair. Jarrod had, so why couldn't he?

He turned to shout at Jarrod. But Jarrod had fallen asleep. He was slumped against a tree, his face against the bark of the trunk, he was snoring quietly. His hands had fallen by his side. And in his lap was the gun.

Sean didn't think twice about taking it.

Five

DAYLIGHT WAS CREEPING through the trees. So was Sean. He carried the gun in a hot fist.

He made his way to a clearing not far from where Jarrod was sleeping. He'd been staring at the gun for ages; now he was going to fire it. He didn't care if Jarrod heard the shot. He rested his back up against a tree and held the pistol out in front of him in both hands. In fact, he wanted Jarrod to hear the shot. He slowly cocked the hammer. He wanted his mum and dad to hear the shot too. Then they'd all know how angry he was. He was breathing heavily.

He pointed the gun into the under-growth. His aim was wild. All he wanted to do was be a cowboy.

'Wild West,' he hissed through gritted teeth.

The world lit up and boomed.

The trees around him burst into life. Startled birds leapt into the sky. The whole wood was suddenly alive. His hands felt as if they'd been slapped, his ears were ringing. He didn't even wait for the thunder around him to fade before he let off another shot. Then another. And another.

The noise was so big and loud, his entire body thudded as if he were

personally discharging the bullets.

He felt as if he'd run a race, he was panting just as badly. He was feeling a bit dizzy. Both of his palms were stinging like crazy. He stood back, waiting for the world to right itself.

The birds finally began to settle, the wood slowly sank back into its morning hush. But something was still moving, something hadn't quite returned to normal. Sean took a tentative step forward and peered through the dim light into the trees. Something was . . .

He had hit something. He saw it collapse to the ground.

'JAZ!' he screamed. 'JAZ! HELP!'

Jarrod had heard the shots. He felt as if

he'd been punched out of his sleep. The woods were a frenzy around him, then Sean had started screaming. Jarrod stumbled to his feet and charged headlong through the trees.

He crashed through the bushes into another clearing and saw Sean ahead. He was on his knees. Had he shot himself?

Then Jarrod saw the deer.

It lay on its side among the nettles and the broken branches. It tried to stand, its legs kicking. Its head shuddered with the effort. Its body heaved for breath. Its white, downy stomach still galloped. A puffy cloud of red was spitting into the air from the red-black hole in its throat. A spasm ripped through its body. He could

hear it gasping. Its eyes wide, wide, white.

'Help me, Jaz,' Sean said. 'Help me lift it up.'

Jarrod stood still. Staring.

'Help me!'

'You hit a deer.'

'I know. I didn't mean to. It was an accident. You've got to help me. Don't let it die. It's got to get up.'

Sweat ran down Sean's face, into his

eyes and mouth. He ran behind the deer and squatted down, pushing his hands underneath its back, its so soft fur on its back. He tried to lift it up, tried to tip it on to its feet. He couldn't lift it up. He couldn't get it on to its feet.

Blood, thick like soup, like a dense gel, covered its snowy-white throat. He could hear it crying. A puffy, red cloud spattering its pelt. It wanted to get up. He

could hear it screaming.

'I can't lift you up. *I can't lift you up*!'

'Put it out of its misery.'

'Help me lift it up.'

'You've got to put it out of its misery.'

'It's got to run away. It's got to get up.'

'Shoot it, Sean. It's in agony.'

'I can't, we've got to . . .'

'Sean! Kill it. Shoot it. Look what you've done to it.'

Sean could hardly see for sweat and tears and hurt and pain.

'Now, Sean. Do it now!'

Holding the gun in front of his chest in both hands, Sean was on his knees, hearing Jarrod sobbing, looking at the deer, seeing what he'd done to the deer, tears burning. Lowering the gun so that the barrel rested gently just above the delicate twitching ear, Sean pulled on the trigger.

Six

'COME ON, SEAN. Leave it now. Let's go.'

Sean had blood on his hands. 'It was an accident,' he sobbed. 'I didn't mean to.'

Jarrod nodded. He helped Sean to his feet. He tried not to look at the deer. 'We'd better go.'

But Sean wouldn't leave. He pulled some broken branches over the dead deer. 'I didn't see it. I didn't even know it was there.' His tears were silent but heavy, running thick lines through the dirt on his face. He turned to look at Jarrod.

'What're we gonna do?' he whispered.

Jarrod shook his head. He didn't know. He felt sick inside. 'We should just go home,' he said.

Sean tried in vain to wipe away his tears. The gun lay in the grass where he'd dropped it. He picked it up.

'I wish you'd never found it,' Jarrod said.

'I just wanted to be a cowboy.' The words caught in Sean's throat.

'Get rid of it,' Jarrod said. 'Throw it away. And come home.'

'But we'll get into trouble.'

Jarrod nodded, then said, 'Maybe they'll be so pleased to see us they'll forget to tell us off.'

'D'you reckon they will?'

Jarrod didn't answer. He was already walking away through the trees.

Sean stared at the gun in his blood-stained hand. It was much too big for him to hold properly, it made his hand look small and childish. But he kept hold of it anyway. He turned and followed Jarrod.

The sun was high, hot and yellow outside the cover of the trees. The young, green field ahead of them dipped in the middle where a pool of hazy mirage-water could be seen. Jarrod led the way, Sean followed, calling to his friend as they walked, 'I'm sorry if I've made trouble for you.' He held the gun down, pointing at the ground. 'I didn't mean to.'

Jarrod didn't answer. He took his coat off and tied it around his waist by the arms.

Sean held his head down. He fiddled with the gun in his hands. 'I could never kill anything again. Honest I couldn't.' He was falling further and further behind Jarrod.

The mirage-water had disappeared by the time they reached it. They walked on towards the hill that overlooked Tallow.

'I meant it when I said I didn't want all this to happen,' Sean called ahead to Jarrod. 'I really didn't.' He'd stopped walking. He passed the gun from hand to hand. Turning it over and around in his grip. 'I've never caused this much trouble before. Never in my life.'

Sean gazed at the gun. He stroked the barrel, played his finger along the trigger.

He looked at Jarrod. He looked at the gun. Back to Jarrod. And to the gun again.

Then he dropped it.

He simply let it fall from his hand. And without looking back he ran to catch up with his friend, heading for home and whatever lay beyond.